RED FOX wakens in the glen

To tiptoe from his forest den

With dreams of chickens in the pen

At Old McCloskey's Farm again.

For my nephew, Peter Jon, who loves the farm. B.H.

For my dad. C.S.

Text copyright © 2006 Brian Heinz

Illustrations copyright © 2006 Chris Sheban

Published in 2006 by Creative Editions

123 South Broad Street, Mankato, MN 56001 USA

Creative Editions is an imprint of The Creative Company.

Designed by Rita Marshall, edited by Aaron Frisch

Printed in Italy

Library of Congress Cataloging-in-Publication Data

Heinz, Brian J., 1946-

Red fox at McCloskey's farm / by Brian Heinz ; illustrator, Chris Sheban.

Summary: Illustrations and rhyming text relate the details of
Red Fox's failed raid of the henhouse at McCloskey's Farm.

ISBN: 978-1-56846-195-3

[1. Red fox—Fiction. 2. Foxes—Fiction. 3. Farm life—Fiction.
4. Stories in rhyme.] I. Sheban, Chris, ill. II. Title.

PZ8.3.H41344Red 2006

[E]—dc22   2005051937

2 4 6 8 9 7 5 3

RED FOX AT McCLOSKEY'S FARM

Written by **BRIAN HEINZ** Illustrated by **CHRIS SHEBAN**

CREATIVE EDITIONS

Veiled in clouds, the moon hangs pale.

Fox licks his chops, he flicks his tail,

And strikes out on familiar trails

Of logs, and streams, and walls of shale.

His ears so sharp, his eyes so bright,

Slender legs race through the night

'Til **RED FOX** spies the farmhouse light.

He stops. The chicken coop's in sight!

Hound Dog's keening in the wind

And spots a shadow, sleek and thin.

Between the corn rows **RED FOX** skims,

A hungry phantom moving in.

But in the shadows Hound Dog waits.

He blinks. He yawns. It's half past eight.

Tonight may seal **RED FOX**'s fate

Before he clears the henhouse gate.

On Hound Dog's face, a twisted scowl,

From Hound Dog's throat, a wicked growl

That rumbles to a mighty howl

And panics all the sleeping fowl.

Candles glow from overhead,

McCloskey thinks it's time for bed,

But hears the uproar and, in dread,

Throws the window up instead.

"Gadzooks, the Fox!" McCloskey swears,

"I'll tear that rascal hide from hair!"

He runs out in his underwear

And trips across the rocking chair.

The henhouse shakes and feathers fly

When **RED FOX** pokes his nose inside,

And roosters, hens, and chicks decide

To flap for cover, run and hide.

McCloskey gathers rocks to clout

RED FOX, who spins and wheels about

To see Ol' Hound Dog's frothing mouth

And hear McCloskey's snarling shouts.

Stumbling as the stones are thrown,

McCloskey stubs his little toe

And dances out a do-si-do

towards the pig sty. Down he goes.

"I've got you now!" McCloskey roars

As mini-boulders by the score

Shatter hinges on the door

And rattle down upon the floor.

RED FOX springs and leaps aside,

But Hound Dog comes in bounding strides

With crushing teeth and jaws stretched wide.

No hens tonight, Red Fox decides.

The cackles and howls, the hooting and shouting,

A crazy-eyed farmer, his Hound Dog a-growling,

It's just not the night for **RED FOX** to be scouting,

And not quite the yard for Red Fox to be prowling.

Time to escape! **RED FOX** has his doubts

Whether it's possible. Where is the route?

Behind him the barking, the shouts all about.

His fear hurls him over the fences. He's out!

Moonglow lights the dew-drenched grass

And McCloskey's muddied face, aghast.

RED FOX yips. The danger's passed.

He's back in the comforting woodlands at last.

RED FOX sleeping in the glen,

Curled up in his cozy den,

With dreams of chickens in the pen,

At Old McCloskey's Farm ... Again.